Beauty Within the Beast

A DARK FANTASY RETELLING

INARA GAGE

SILVER CORD MARKETING

*To everyone who feels a little more at peace every time they pick up a
book, regardless of the crazy ride we take you on.
The more insane it is, the saner we feel.*

Trigger Warning:

This novella includes depictions of sexual assault (SA) involving a character who is not of mature age. It also features sexual content, including masturbation and explicit descriptions of sexual acts, along with graphic language and violence. This work is intended for mature audiences only. Please note, this list is not exhaustive, and other potentially triggering topics or situations may appear without additional warning. Your well-being is important, and your mental health matters. Reader discretion is advised.

Chapter One

STEELE

THE RAIN BEATS down in relentless sheets, each droplet like an icy needle against Steele's skin, mirroring the desperate, cold grip of the village's despair. He swings his sword wildly, and with each labored grunt, he cuts through a tiny section of the gnarled brambles and thorny bushes shrouding the long-forgotten path. The blade catches on branches, snapping them like brittle bones, the sounds being swallowed by the storm. This path—this forbidden stretch of forest—has haunted his childhood like a shadow, whispered of in fireside tales meant to keep wandering boys from testing its dark embrace.

The woods are a coagulation of ancient, decrepit trees, their twisted forms clawing skyward as if begging for salvation. The rumors told of ghostly wails, of creatures lurking just beyond sight, of those who entered but never returned. Steele remembers laughing at those stories once, fearless in his youth. But now, the chill crawling up his spine is far from childish terror.

Desperate times call for desperate measures.

His family hasn't eaten in days. The thought of his little sister's hollow cheeks and his mother's trembling hands push him onward. Ever since the death of his beloved father, Steele has taken on the burden of making sure his mother and sister eat and are cared for.

If the rumors are true, and there *is* something hidden in this cursed forest—a treasure, a beast with a bounty on its head, anything—then he has no choice but to find it. Starvation is the only thing more certain than the danger awaiting him in the shadows.

Another swing, another spray of broken thorns, and the path opens slightly. The forest yawns before him, its heart an abyss of flickering shadows and suffocating silence.

Steele takes a shaky breath, gripping his sword tighter.

There's no turning back now.

Years ago, a mysterious blight swept across the land, leaving crops to rot in the fields and the soil barren. The sickness spread from plants to livestock, wiping out the kingdom's once-prosperous farmlands. The villagers called it the Plague of Withering, believing it to be a curse brought on by the king's greed.

The once beloved king, rumored to be a sorcerer, vanished into the night after a bitter fallout with the queen. Many whispered that he cursed the land as vengeance, stripping it of fertility and prosperity. His departure divided the court, made the people resentful, and left the queen broken.

The queen sought to secure resources, distract her people from their suffering, and waged an ill-advised war against a neighboring kingdom. The conflict drained the treasury, weakened the army, and left the borders vulnerable. When the army returned in defeat, the kingdom's coffers were empty, and its enemies circled like wolves.

The ancient forest bordering the court, long a source of myth and fear, began encroaching on farmlands and roads. The villagers believe it's alive, reclaiming what was stolen from it centuries ago when the kingdom expanded its territory. Tales of eerie whispers and vanishing hunters spread, keeping even the bravest from venturing too far.

Sensing weakness, the nobles began hoarding their little

wealth and resources, turning on each other to secure their survival. The royal family's influence diminished, leaving the villages to fend for themselves. Bandits roamed freely, preying on the vulnerable and plunging the kingdom into chaos.

The kingdom had once thrived under the blessings of its deity, but as suffering spread, temples were abandoned and priests silenced. The people began to believe they were forsaken, their prayers unanswered. Some turned to forbidden magicks or the forest's dark whispers, further dividing the land's fragile unity.

All of these calamities culminated in what the people now call the Great Hunger. With the land barren and the treasury empty, starvation swept the kingdom. Families like Steele's, once modest but self-sufficient, now faced the unbearable choice of watching loved ones waste away or venturing into danger for scraps of survival.

Once a shining beacon of prosperity, the kingdom now exists as a husk of its former self, its people held together only by the faint hope that something—*anything*—might save them from the abyss.

The calluses burn his hands as he strikes another row of thorns in front of him, his skin bloody and scratched from doing this for hours in the rain. The only thing keeping him going is the thought that whatever lies behind this miles-wide thicket of thorns has to be better than what he's leaving behind.

The sky has darkened due to the bloated black clouds blotting out the sun, and his stomach rumbles in protest to the exertion he's emitting to rid the path of these cursed vines. The rain has been falling in fits and starts throughout the whole day, and he hasn't rested since he woke up this morning.

It's been five days since he set off into the forbidden forest; his mother, sister, and other family and friends waved him off into the depths of despair he's now in.

Many others have tried and failed to fell these woods, to get as far as they could and discover there is actually an end to them, but every man, woman, and child who has ventured too far into this dark and forbidden place either haven't returned, or haven't returned the same.

There are also rumors dating back to the Great Hunger—hundreds of years of folklore—telling a tale of something so wicked living at the edge of the forest, so wicked indeed that it killed every living tree within a hundred-mile radius.

Tales of what or who this evil is has been lost to time, warping and wafting with every new version. They're so distorted and aged that no one knows the origin or if the rumors have even an inkling of truth.

No one knows.

Anyone who's made it to the end of the dead trees has never returned to tell the tale.

However, it is going to change for Steele.

He will be triumphant and bring back a valuable treasure that will be worth his weight in gold.

He will be the savior of Wyndhallow.

Exhaustion blurs his vision as he stops and rests on the trunk of a large tree, unhooking his canteen from his belt and taking two large swigs. He had filled the canteen up this morning by the babbling brook he'd made camp by, boiling the water before funneling it into his container.

The few berries he'd found weren't much to quell the ache in his gut from the hunger pangs but he knew, more than anything else, that he was close to uncovering something.

He can feel it.

Capping the canteen, he wipes his beard with his gloved hand, removing the sweat, rain, and spittle before continuing.

Chop, chop, swing. Chop, chop, swing.

The rhythm of his blade bites through the thick vines as the last remnants of daylight fade, swallowed by the encroaching darkness. His vision diminishes in the dimming light, and the cold rain soaks him to the bone. Just as he considers giving up for the night, a sound stops him mid-swing.

Music.

"No," he mutters to himself, shaking his head. *It can't be. I must be imagining things.*

He cocks his head, straining to hear beyond the drumming rain. The faint notes of a lute weaves through the wind—or so he thinks. But then, just as quickly, the melody shifts into the harsh caw of a distant bird echoing beyond the craggy woods.

He exhales sharply, gripping his sword tighter. Then it comes again—the unmistakable melody, light, and teasing, pulling at something deep inside him.

This time, he knows he isn't imagining it.

Adrenaline surges through his veins. He swings faster, slashing at the tangled brambles with newfound desperation. Each vine feels like a prison, keeping him from salvation—or maybe insanity. He isn't sure which. His breath comes in ragged gasps as he hacks away, driven by something he can't explain.

Then, through the choking mass of vines, a faint, shimmering red light pulses in the darkness.

He throws his head back and laughs at the rain, a wild, unhinged sound that echoes through the air. Whether it's relief, madness, or some cruel joke of exhaustion, he doesn't know. But he keeps going.

Six more layers.

Five.

Four.

Three.

Two.

One.

Finally, the last of the vines fall away, and the sight before him steals his breath.

Lightning cracks the sky, and Steele narrows his eyes ahead of him against the sting of the rainfall.

A magnificent rose garden yawns in the hallow, glowing faintly in the stormy night. It's like a labyrinth of life and fire, with intricately shaped hedges depicting fantastical creatures, their forms illuminated by the soft, pulsing light of thousands of roses, lilies, lotus, and daffodils—all made of fire.

In the heart of the garden, atop a grand fountain, stands the largest lotus, glowing a brilliant red and crackling with flames. As he steps closer, he swears he hears it whisper.

"Pluck me," it beckons. "Pluck me, and you'll never go hungry again. Cut me down, and I'll turn to gold. Sell me, and you'll be richer than kings."

"No, pick me!" another flower screams, its voice seductive and honeyed. "I bring eternal youth and boundless love to anyone who keeps me."

The whispers grow louder, an intoxicating symphony that clouds his thoughts.

Drawn in, his hand trembles as he reaches for the largest flower. The whispers swell, promising salvation, wealth, and love. His blade lifts, ready to sever the stem and claim his prize.

But just as the blade begins to descend—

The world goes black.

Chapter Two

THE BEAST

Darkness has become my playground, that comfort blanket in the darkest night. It's the only thing keeping my anger company that my rage finds solace in.

All the other emotions have come and died upon my sorrow.

Time has no measure. Though the sun comes and goes, sprouts and dies daily, the stars and moon and nothingness wilt and blossom in days that feel like seconds.

Every memory I used to have has faded into the dust of this place. Fragments of my broken mind relinquish bouts of sadness here and there, but for the most part, it's my anger keeping me warm, my rage for what was taken from me sharpening my jagged edges.

I can't even remember what I used to look like, and though this form feels comfortable, I can't bear to see myself.

Every mirror in the Gothic mansion has been covered.

And while the sun seems to rise and fall often, no light touches the grounds.

Hecate Manor has been the place I've been bound to for longer than I know how to measure. Filled with dark furnishings, every wall is painted black with red accents.

The clang of the trap outside is what roused me awake.

It's been a long time since I've had a decent meal.

Slipping out of bed, the patchwork of my skin and fur glimmers golden from the candlelight, shimmering and catching the light like a predator in shadow.

Caw! Caw!

Quill, my raven, swoops in from the open window.

I sweep my robe over myself, covering my gnarled fur and hold out my hand, the long black talons stretching out to the darkness. "Hello pretty girl. Come to mama."

Quill's silver-tipped feathers glisten as she cascades toward me, landing on my outstretched finger. "In shadowed halls, I dwell alone, my name unknown, my fate my own. My captor's heart is cold as stone, yet power is mine, mine to atone. Though walls confine, my spirits fly, my voice is soft, but never die, release me, and the truth is clear, but at a cost, you'll learn to fear. What am I?"

"Oh, bird your riddles will be the death of me."

I kiss her on the beak and release her. She flies out the room and into the house.

"We have company," I announce to the ghosts.

The air feels heavy as I glide down the sprawling staircase, the flickering candles cast shadows that crawl along the walls. My talons click against the polished black-wood steps, a sound that echoes through the silence. Quill's riddle gnaws at the edges of my mind; each word laced with an ominous truth I'm not yet ready to decipher.

The trap outside.

I haven't seen a soul brave the forest in years—not since the stories of what lurks here grew teeth sharper than any warning. My hunger stirs a pang that makes my chest tighten. It's been so long since I've fed properly. My rage sharpens it, fueling my steps as I cross the grand hall.

The house does what it can to keep me fed, producing magick breads, cheeses, and stews, but meat is something it cannot give me and I am in need of a delicious, juicy steak or even something else for the manor to put into the soup.

I am sick to death of bone broth and carrots.

The manor creaks as though it, too, is curious. The chandeliers sway slightly in the draft of unseen winds, and the painted eyes of long-forgotten ancestors seem to follow me. Quill perches on a rail above, her silver-tipped feathers catching the dim glow as her dark eyes glitter with mischief—or perhaps, foreboding.

I reach the iron-bolted door that leads to the outer grounds. The trap lies just beyond, hidden among the thorn-covered maze that encircles the manor like a crown of despair. My heart quickens as I grip the cold iron handle.

What waits for me beyond this door? Prey to satisfy my hunger, or something far worse? Something that might remember what I was before I forgot myself.

With a deep breath, I swing the door open. The rain pours in sheets, thick and unyielding, drenching the ground into sludge. The world beyond the garden's boundaries is hidden, shrouded in mist and darkness. But the trap...

There, tangled in the iron jaws, is no ordinary animal. It's a man, ragged and bleeding, his breathing shallow but determined. His face is pale from the blood loss, yet his eyes—piercing and defiant—lock with mine. Something flashes there, something unnerving.

"Help me," he rasps, his voice breaking the heavy silence.

I step forward, the rain soaking through my robe as I crouch over him. My talons hover just above his face, and for a moment, I see myself reflected in his wide terrified eyes.

The beast. The monster. The forgotten.

"Why did you come here?" My voice is a low growl, more animal than human.

He flinches but doesn't look away. "My family...they're starving."

My anger stirs at his answer. It's been so long since I've had something to destroy. But beneath the fury, something else flickers—a faint ember of curiosity. What is he doing here?

Quill caws from her perch, her riddle echoing in my thoughts. *Release me, and the truth is clear, but at a cost, you'll learn to fear.*

I bare my fangs in a snarl, but something stays my hand. I lean closer.

"What would you give," I whisper, "to save them?"

The silence stretches into eternity, mixing with the thunder and the pelting rain.

"Anything," he utters, so soft I almost swear I didn't hear him say it at all.

I pace around him, thinking of what it would mean to send him back to Wyndhallow.

I've been persecuted in witch hunts before.

One of the many things that led me to the darkness I live in now.

That was hundreds of years ago.

The whispers and rumors of the phantom I've become have long ago been covered by dirt and dust and grime, fading into nursery rhymes of the past.

I turn to go, to leave him to die in my garden.

"Wait!" he shouts, and I stop at the archway hedge. "I'll do anything. Please."

Anger floods me.

I rush at him, one quick and deafening maneuver of strength and wit and fury, nearly stomping on his head as he lies on the ground where the fountain caved in and the trap came out. The trap, with my most precious and haunting and enchanting bloom, to ensnare antelopes and bears and elk—anything with meat.

Never a human.

Nay, never a human man.

He flinches as I raise my taloned foot to stomp him out of his misery.

How dare he come here and threaten my existence!

How fucking dare he cripple my wards and trample my garden, attempting to steal from me!

"You were going to steal from me! What, were you just going to take the enchanted flower back to your village and sell it to the highest bidder? What happens to me then? When they find out where you got it from? And then you tell them of what you saw, only for them to come trampling through my grounds to tie me up and kill me, too? To sell me to some freak-show circus? How does that help me?"

Wincing in pain, he tries to move his legs, which are trapped in the jaws. "I won't! I won't tell them anything of what I saw. Please. Just let me go. I'll leave here and never return."

I lower my leg and scratch my chin, the talon thick and cool and coaxing against my angry skin.

Again I go to leave when Ryx pops out from behind one of the hedges.

My mischievous and sometimes irksome raccoon who's bound to the grounds as much as I.

"You could always strike a bargain with him," Ryx says, standing on his hind legs and plucking an apple from the tree above him.

I quirk my brows. "Strike a deal?"

Biting into the apple, he says, "Yes. Give him money to send home as long as he stays here with you on the grounds." Bits of apple fly out of his mouth as he speaks.

"What good would that do? What would that give me?"

His mouth quirks up in a smirk. "Companionship, m'lady. And dick."

I nearly choke on my own spit. I grab him by the tuft of fur behind his neck and wing him up to face me. "No man in their right mind would ever have sex with a beast like me," I snarl.

He tosses the apple and pets the side of my face. "Oh my dear sweet Reverie." He leans in close to my ear to whisper the next part. "If you get him to see the beauty within the beast, our curse will forever be broken."

I think on that thought for a few seconds before setting him back down.

He's right.

This could be my chance to break the curse for good.

I amble back over to him and kneel down. "Okay, I have a proposition for you."

His rich, amber-colored eyes set behind dark lashes peer up at me."Anything."

"Stay here with me. I'll give you money and food to send home. But there's one condition."

His nose crinkles as he scrunches his eyebrows together. "What?"

"You can never leave."

He blinks slowly, pondering his choice. "What's the other option?"

A wicked smile seeps between my teeth. "Death."

Chapter Three

STEELE

"You must say the words before I release you," Reverie tells Steele, circling the man lying in the trap.

"What words?" he asks, a pained groan grating up his throat as he tries to move his legs.

"Submit to never leaving. You must say the words so the magick takes hold. Lest you wish to stay here and die of blood loss, starvation, and hypothermia."

The pain in his leg has morphed into something in an entirely new realm of agony, one without a word for it yet. His head is pounding, yet he feels light-headed and woozy, and the soaking wet clothes sticking to his skin feel like a thousand pounds.

He'll do anything just to get somewhere warm with something to eat.

"Yes, I submit. I agree to never leave the grounds."

With the words uttered through his lips, the trap snaps open and fades back into the ground. The lotus flower rises up again with the fountain, and Steele rolls to the side to avoid being stuck atop it. The light from the flower gleams so brightly that the rain falling in his eyes turns to bright glowing orbs. Pain in his legs from the trap's teeth fades, and in a blast of shockingly warm and intense light, he shields his eyes lest he goes blind.

When he opens them again, he's in a black four-poster bed with black furnishings and drapes that are closed, yet soft light sneaks in through the cracks.

Shoving the fluffy black comforter off, he examines his legs—which are bare—in search of any sign of the awful wound the trap left.

Nothing.

His skin is untouched.

Rubbing his eyes and scratching his head, he stands from the bed to investigate the chambers he woke up in.

If it weren't for the eerily strange place, he would've thought he was in some sort of fever dream, but as he makes it to the window and opens the drapes, the sprawling maze of hedges with the fire flower atop the fountain confirms it is absolutely real.

A draft crawls up his legs, and when he looks down, he realizes he is not wearing a lick of clothing.

Covering his middle portion, he ambles to the closet to find something to wear.

Surprisingly, pants and shirts all his size occupy the wardrobe.

As he pulls on a white shirt and black pants, he wonders who brought him here to this room and who took off all his clothes.

A hunger pang rumbles in his stomach, and he applies pressure, hoping it will lessen the pain until he can find some food.

The great oak doors to his room open with a creak and slam closed behind him with a hollow thud. His bare feet slap the cold, black stone of the manor stairs while he makes his way to the foyer for something to eat.

The vaulted ceiling looms high overhead in the grand foyer, adorned with chandeliers dripping black crystals that catch the dim light and fracture it into fleeting rainbows on the polished marble floor. The air here is thick, silent in a way that presses against his ears, making him acutely aware of his heartbeat.

An elderly man with a skeletal frame and a black suit that fits too well for comfort steps forward. His pale blue eyes linger on him for a moment longer than necessary before he speaks.

"Sir," the man intones, his voice a low, gravelly echo in the cavernous space. "You are to remain on the west wing of the estate. Attempting to go elsewhere or leave will...not end well."

"Who are you?" Steele queries, taking a cautious step back.

"I am Edmund, sir. The manor's butler."

Steel stiffens, his fingers curling into his palms. "Well, Edmund, I was only looking for food; I wasn't trying to leave."

Edmund's lips curl into something resembling a smile but devoid of warmth. "I'll show you back to your room and have something sent up."

A flicker of movement at the top of the sweeping staircase leading to the east wing draws Steele's gaze. His eyes rake across the massive foyer and the landing of the east wing. A portrait of a woman—young, delicate, with a cascade of sable locks—watches him from the shadows of her frame. Her eyes, dark blue and sharp, seemingly narrow on him before slipping back to looking straight ahead. "What's up there?" he asks as he follows the man back toward the way he came.

"You're forbidden from entering the east wing," Edmund continues as though Steele hadn't spoken. "It's a matter of the utmost importance."

Steele frowns. "Why?"

The butler tilts his head, considering him. "It's not your concern. Shall I show you to your room?"

His every instinct tells him to turn around, to press back through those heavy doors, and to disappear into the forest he had come from. But the doors, massive and ancient, are already sealed shut. And he feels that the manor wouldn't let him leave even if he tried.

"Fine," Steele mutters, his voice barely above a growl.

The butler gestures with a thin hand. "Follow me."

They ascend the grand staircase to the west, passing by heavy, embroidered tapestries that depict scenes of war and ruin. The house shifts as they move, its hallways bending in subtle ways that make no sense. When they reach the west wing, where Steele's quarters lay, he can no longer tell how far he is from the foyer or even the hallway he originally came from.

At last, the butler stops in front of a door with iron fittings. "This is your room. Dinner is served promptly at eight in the main dining hall. I suggest you not be late."

Steele steps inside again without another word, and the door slams shut behind him.

That was pointless.

His hunger still haunts him.

He sits on the bed and looks around the simple room, yet larger than any place he'd ever slept. The bed is canopied, its dark velvet curtains heavy and still. A fire crackles in the hearth, though he hadn't seen anyone light it.

But something about the woman in the painting and the cold dismissal of the east wing gnaws at him.

He lets out a long breath, dropping his eyes to his hands.

He is trapped here.

Chapter Four

STEELE

WITHOUT CLOCKS—WHICH he noticed were missing from the manor along with the mirrors—he had no concept of time but would wager nearly an hour passed before someone brought him lunch.

There was a tap on the door, but there was no evidence of who had knocked. He opened the door to a tray of stew and bread paired with a pewter mug filled with ale.

He'd inhaled the soup and swallowed the bread in one bite, and when the ale was gone, it magickally refilled itself.

He napped until dinner, then ate alone at the table fit for a castle, returning to his room for more ale.

Days—nay weeks—have passed like this, where nothing has changed.

He'd nearly been killed multiple times by different things in the manor and on the grounds.

The sentient shadows that linger in the dark corners will likely claim his sanity first. They strike when the lights are dim, suffocating, or slashing with razor-like tendrils.

The furniture is haunted. Chairs, armoires, or chandeliers spring to life when least expected, trapping or crushing anything too close.

The grand staircase subtly shifts its steps, leading him into traps or void-like falls into darkness if he isn't too careful. Every time it happens, he wakes in bed like it was all a dream.

Portraits on the walls seem to follow him, and when provoked —or ignored too long, the figures inside claw their way into reality to attack.

Occasionally, entire rooms shift into dangerous spaces—the sitting room becomes an inferno, and a hallway grows barbed branches with a hunger for flesh.

On the grounds, thorned vines and flowering plants lure him with sweet scents and promises of freedom before snapping shut like jaws. The gardens are ever-changing, trapping him in endless loops or leading him into traps—bottomless pits, spiked hedges, or drowning bogs. Specific patches of ground liquefy without warning, pulling him into suffocating mud or icy water, and the stone gargoyles or animal figures seemingly come to life at night.

The manor shifts walls and floors, trapping him in shrinking spaces or rooms that become a place of nightmares, with ghostly apparitions of people he once loved and lost and some he's never seen or doesn't know.

He hasn't seen or heard from the beast since he's been here, though he seems to think she haunts the paintings. Sometimes, he swears she's behind him, and then there's no one there.

There was the one time in the middle of the night he saw her roaming the grounds from his window, Edmund on her tail, so he snuck over to her wing.

It was terrifying.

Everything in her bedchamber was clawed to bits, and large gouges scarred every surface made of wood.

He never wants to venture to that side ever again.

Today, lunch consists of cheese and crackers, and he finishes it off with five to six refills of ale before he sets out on his daily exploring.

As dangerous as the manor is and unreliable with staying the same, it's the only thing he's found to keep him occupied and not anxiety-ridden about spending the rest of his life here.

Maybe he should have accepted his death.

Satisfied for now—and a little buzzed—he leaves the tray on the right side of the door and stalks off down the dark hallway.

So far, in his exploring and near-death experiences, he's found multiple bedrooms, nooks and crannies with reading chairs and tables, countless bathrooms, two storage cubbies, six stately sitting rooms, and a massive library fit for a king.

Reading is one of his favorite pastimes, and so today, he climbs the ladder to the second level and picks one. Tome in hand, he sits in the chair next to the fire and opens the book.

Books are magickal things. Black ink on dead trees spins wild hallucinations in their holders' minds.

Steele flips another page, engrossed in the tale. The warmth of the fire at his side pairs perfectly with the faint buzz of ale still coursing through him. The book in his hand—a weathered classic whose pages feel like silk beneath his fingers—pulls him deeper into its world. He runs his thumbs over a passage, marveling again at how ink on paper could create entire universes.

Books *are* magick.

The snap of wood in the hearth startles him, and he glances up, only to find he's no longer alone.

She stands in the doorway, one shoulder pressing into the frame. The firelight softens her beastly form, making the glint of her blue eyes less predatory and more contemplative. She doesn't speak; she just watches him, her presence both imposing and oddly comforting.

"You like books?" she asks or states, her tone is unreadable.

Steele sits up straighter, instinctively bristling at being caught in a rare moment of peace.

"I do," he says simply, closing the book but keeping a finger in its spine. "They're one of the few places a man like me can escape."

There's a twitch to her lips—not quite a smile, but not

entirely devoid of amusement. She steps into the room, her clawed feet making little noise on the polished floor. "Escape from what?"

Thick, bushy brows raise to his hairline. "From people like you."

There's a flicker in her expression—hurt? No, it's too brief to be certain. "And yet, here you are," she replies, moving closer. "In *my* library. Reading *my* books."

Glancing down at the large book in his lap, he strokes its worn cover. "They're the only things here that don't seem to want to kill me."

The laugh she cradles is low and bitter. "You assume much, warrior. Not everything in this manor is your enemy."

He tilts his head, studying her. "Are you saying you're not my enemy?"

The claws at her side twitch, and for a moment, she looks away as if she doesn't trust herself to answer. Instead, she changes the subject. "You've chosen that one."

Following her gaze to the book, he says, "A classic," trying to sound nonchalant.

"It was one of her favorites," she murmurs, almost too softly.

Steele stiffens. "The woman in the painting?"

She nods, her gaze distant, as if caught between memory and regret. "She believed books held answers even when the world didn't. I think that's why she...why I..." She stops, her voice catching,

"You miss her," he says, surprising even himself with the gentleness in his tone.

Her head snaps toward him, her eyes narrowing. "Don't presume to know me."

Raising his hands in mock surrender, he leans back in his chair. "I'm not. But I know what it's like to lose someone."

The room grows quieter, and the fire's crackle fills the space between them. She studies him for a long moment, her beastly features softening, the sharp edges dulled by something he can't quite name.

"And what did you do with that loss?" she asks, her voice like a ribbon of silk, soft to the touch, but if you turn it on its side, it'll slice you to the bone.

He swallows hard, gripping the book tighter. "I carried it. Still do. Some weights never leave. They're like boulders that stack inside you, making moving hard."

For the first time, her condemning gaze doesn't pierce him. Instead, it rests on him, heavy with an understanding that unnerves him like a kick to the ribs—winding him. Chest deflating.

"You surprise me," she says finally.

"And you terrify me," he admits.

Her lips curve—an almost smile, fleeting but real. "Good."

But as she turns to leave, he calls after her. "Does that mean you're not my enemy?"

She pauses in the doorway, her clawed hand on the frame. Her answer, when it comes, is cryptic and laced with something unspoken. "You'll have to decide that for yourself."

"Reverie," he calls the name he'd heard a portrait whisper late one night while exploring.

When she turns again, her dark blue eyes narrow as though he's stepping close to an edge he shouldn't linger near.

A low growl creeps up her throat, "Tread carefully, man."

"Steele," he tells her and waits for her to allow him to continue. "What happened to you?"

Before he knows what happened, she's upon him, holding him aloft by her claws, the sharp talons stabbing him in the neck. "Don't. Ever. Ask. That. Again."

Breath flees his lungs, and he waits for death to claim him. Her breath is hot on his cheek, and her blue eyes are even with his.

And yet, inside those rage-filled eyes, he sees that woman in the portrait, cowering inside the beast who's claimed her life.

What curse would lock a beautiful woman such as she inside a ravenous beast?

Chapter Five

REVERIE

I HOLD my breath hostage as I flee his wing and make it back to mine.

For weeks, I've studied him. I've watched him succeed in the manor's nefarious games—at tends to want to kill anything that may one day free me from my curse—and he's surpassed all my expectations of him.

He's strong and fierce, yet gentle and kind.

He's known loss—far more significant than I can fathom—even though I can't remember who I lost.

The ghosts of something I can scarcely grasp have corpses anchored to my subconscious. The place inside me where that woman exists is vast, yet she lingers there, bleeding and bloody and clinging to my skeleton.

And when I held him aloft in my talons and my lungs pulled full of his scent, his piercing eyes, rich with the molten color of firewood, skewered me, and I swear he saw the girl within.

I've been so mad, hardened, and scrupulous for longer than my memory stretches, but I know there is not much left that's soft and tender in my heart. It's hostile and hardened and looks for war, even when peace is presented as a gorgeous man reading one of my favorite books. It's usually impervious to things like caring, which is a dangerous territory, no matter how far my mind drifts. The harder you care for something, the more fragile the world becomes.

All the other times I've watched him—seen him fall victim to the manor's moving rooms, enchanted furniture, and monsters in the garden—tonight I could not fight approaching him any longer.

While the monsters of the manor are real and should be frightening, they are the only things I've had for company in what feels like centuries.

But tonight... tonight, I watched him climb the ladder and pull down one of my favorite books. I witnessed him sit in my favorite chair and get lost in the world that's cradled me in my darkest hour. His thick and calloused fingers strummed the pages like a guitar, and his beard, adding a rugged texture to his already robust appearance, jostled as he moved his lips to mouth the words—a sign of dyslexia—exactly like me.

It was at that moment I glimpsed a flaw, effortlessly beautiful amid the immense energy radiating off him, pressing against me with such intensity that it stole the air from my lungs. When he spoke, his voice—dense and unyielding—pierced through my soul like flint striking stone, scattering sparks that crackled through my icy veins in the most unsettling way.

I pace around my chambers, rage warring with want and the desire to dissect these thoughts. The rage doesn't want company. It takes up too much room in my being for fickle, silly feelings such as lust and desire.

My talons itch to shred the black drapes even more, though ninety percent are nearly shredded to bits. The manor waits until there's no more fabric on the rods before it replaces them with new ones.

"Why don't you just ask him to dinner?" Edmund asks, my butler bringing me my nightly elixir—and right on time.

Whatever he puts in here always calms me down.

I swipe the pewter goblet off the silver tray and slam back the icy cold liquid, wiping my face with the fuzz on my arms. "What?!" I question him, pushing the mug back onto the tray with such force that it buckles his knees a bit.

"You're clearly thinking of him," he states, treading carefully as he edges toward the exit. "It's been longer than I can recall where you've had another young person to talk to. Your childhood was filled with—"

"ENOUGH!" I shout, and he shrinks away from me, my voice gravelly and low, soaked with the beast within. "I don't need you to tell me about me, Edmund."

"Yes, m'lady, I know, it's just—"

"Edmund!" I shout, falling to all fours as my hackles rise.

He taps the tray, and the mug fills, and he sets it on the ground in front of me.

I've hurt Edmund before. Though he's not of this earth, he is more like a living embodiment of my love and warmth, guilt and sorrow, and some shame and grief. He's all the little bits of me I don't have left. Edmund came to be of the things I have discarded.

My claws can still cut him, my words slice into him, and my cold indifference to the world chips away at the armor he's created by being near me for so long.

I can still see the scars.

And he's quick to remind me I have good pieces still tethered to the broken bits of me.

But he is also quick to dampen my mood whenever I have a good day.

It's like he tries to be the balance.

Or both the hero and the villain.

He is both the calm and chaos in my bones.

I drink the elixir, and it's scorching this time, the red-hot sting of the alcohol singes my bones, calms my rage, and settles my soul.

"Invite him to dinner," he says softly, crouching to level me with his heather gray eyes.

I roll my neck to release the tension; it pops in response as my gaze returns to his.

"This is your chance, Rev. You mustn't waste this opportunity, as it may be the only one of its kind."

"You don't know that," I retort, pulling myself up from leaning on all fours.

"You forget I'm the keeper of your lost memories and things you choose to forget."

I open my mouth to say something to get him to stop, and then I close it again. Instead, I turn and move over to the fireplace, even though his words chase me like the flick of a whip.

Edmund straightens from the crouch he'd been in, pulling the mug from the floor with him. "While you may forget the person who cast the spell and the words that bind us, I cannot. They haunt me every second." He reaches me at the fireplace. Mug filled once again, he hands it to me, the amber liquid sloshing up the sides. His cool, gray eyes impale me. "I know you're scared. You confuse that emotion with anger. Set your wrath aside. If you get someone to see the real you inside of this—" he jabs his finger into my upper arm, "we will all be free. And then you can have your vengeance on the real person who deserves it."

His words encircle me, gathering the rest of my rage and laying it to rest for the night. Calm, soothing air picks up the heavy burden that revenge and wrath creates, extinguishing the fire marrow cascading within me. The chilling balm settles me, and I release a ragged and deep breath.

"What if he doesn't like what's left of that girl?" I ask, keeping my lip steady though it nearly threatens to tremble.

"Beneath this big scary beast, you really are a great person Rev. You got dealt a shitty hand and pissed off the wrong person—"

I shove my finger in his face to shut him up. "Tsk tsk. You know I don't—"

He shrugs me off. "Want me to say anything about who you were? I know."

I nod and turn away.

I'm exhausted from this conversation, and we barely talked. I know he's right. Yet I have no desire to gather any bits of me he feels like giving back.

I'm comfortable in my oblivion.

I say nothing as he clears his throat.

"I'll tell him to be promptly at eight."

I give an imperceptible nod and fall into a trance with the flames as he saunters off, leaving the conversation at that.

The doors to my chamber clang closed, and I sink into the chair by the fire, letting the rest of my anger slip into the embers.

I must be on my best behavior for dinner.

Gotta convince a man I'm neither maiden nor monster, but something in between.

Chapter Six

STEELE

Steele stands under the shower, the announcement of tonight's dinner with Reverie still fresh in his mind; as peculiar and intriguing as this experience is, what strikes him most is how her gaze cleaves into his soul. He's never encountered someone whose eyes hold so much battle, a silent war etched into their depths. Her voice, heavy with the weight of heartbreak, carries a tone that seems to echo through centuries. He kicks himself for prying into her past, determined now to push the thought from his mind.

It was just hard not to focus on her with the giant erection he's been sporting since she almost killed him in the library.

He wants to know her story.

Even through her beastly facade, he can sense the woman underneath.

The woman in the portrait was stunning, thick, ravenous.

Deep blue eyes the color of a midnight ocean pierced outward from a long and elegant face. Her inky locks are a fall of curls resting beside her pretty features. The portrait boasted a large-breasted woman in a dark blue dress, the heave of tits so enormous it's hard to focus on anything else.

And the beast who's taken her hostage.

Blue eyes stare at him like beacons in a stormy sea, moonlight mixed within the waves, like frayed threads of a shooting star was unraveled by a hurricane.

Her breasts are still enormous in her beastly form, and the clothing she wore earlier reflected her conflicted identity, mixing remnants of her former life with the raw, untamed nature of her curse.

She wore a flowing, tattered gown that clung to her beastly form, torn and burned in places from her own torment. Her jewelry made of sharp, natural elements—a necklace of obsidian and cuffs twisted in silver—adorned her, adding to her air of primal regality.

Trying to push back against the thoughts, his head full of visions he can't seem to shake away, he tries to focus on showering. His dick throbs as he washes his hair, pulsating as he rinses. Rivulets of water slide over his chilled chest, cascading over his abs and falling beside the tower looming between his legs.

When he can't help but slide his hand down his massive erection, he thinks of her, wondering what it would be like to get tangled up in the sheets together.

Both the beast and the maiden turn him on.

He could picture her kneeling before him in the shower, her gorgeous lips beholden to her fangs wrapping around his cock and sinking the whole thing into her throat.

He has always known he's well endowed, and most women he's been with have never been able to throat the whole thing.

But he has the feeling Reverie could take it in its entirety and not even gag.

Though sometimes gagging is hot.

He lathers soap onto his cock and thrusts his fist erratically, thinking of both the beast and the maiden riding him, those giant boobs bouncing in his face.

He'd take those tits and mouth them ferociously, nibbling and biting, causing a little sting.

As he imagines the sounds she'd make as he bit down, an

explosion of cum shoots out and coats the shower wall. The release came swiftly, yet no less hot and freeing simultaneously.

It's been a long time since he's been with a woman.

Since his wife died in childbirth—both she and the infant—he hasn't been with many women. Though his libido has been in overdrive since he turned twenty-five, he's found little comfort in meaningless sex. And no one has come close to being his next wife.

While the thought of fucking Reverie in beast form is a little unsettling—she could tear him limb from limb in one swipe—it also turned him on like he's never been before.

Although he just came, his dick is already getting hard again at the thought of her.

He tries his hardest to ignore the pulsating cock, finishing his shower and drying off. It's still hard when he puts on the trousers from the wardrobe and does his best to tuck it under his belt.

But with a penis as large as his, it's already awkward to maneuver when it's soft. When it's hard—it's incredibly difficult to hide it.

When he arrives at dinner, she's seated at the far end of the massive table.

Edmund shows him to his seat at the opposite end, and he sits timidly, moving carefully to keep his dick tucked in his belt.

She's already eating the salad when Edmund goes over to the tray and puts a portion of the same salad in front of him.

Steele clears his throat, trying not to look at her for too long. "Thanks for, uh, having me down here tonight. I wasn't sure what to expect."

Reverie uses the utensils to cut a tomato with deliberate precision, her blue eyes briefly flittering to his. "Consider it a gesture of hospitality. Rare as they may be here."

He nervously adjusts his posture. "Right. Well, it's appreciated. Though I'd be lying if I said I wasn't curious...about you.... and this place."

Reverie pauses mid-chew and sets her fork down slowly. "Curiosity is a dangerous thing, Steele. Especially here."

He smirks slightly, trying to lighten the mood. "Good thing I've always been reckless, then. Got me this far, didn't it?"

Full lips twitch in a near-untarnished smile, but it hardens. "And yet, you're still here. Alive. For now."

Steele leans forward slightly. "For now? Is that a threat?"

"It's reality," Reverie answers, her voice sharpening, though he can almost sense a flicker of vulnerability. "You should be more concerned about the things outside this room than me."

"I'm concerned about you, too." He takes a forkful of salad and puts it in his mouth. "The way you look at me sometimes... it's like you're carrying a weight so heavy, it's breaking you apart."

A cold laugh escapes her. "You think you've figured me out? From a few glances? You don't know anything, Steele."

"Maybe not. But I want to." He swallows the salad with a sip of ale. "Why hide everything behind riddles and beastly snarls? You're more than that. I can see it."

Her hands clench the table's edges, her voice lowering to a growl. "You don't know what you're talking about. You sit there, oblivious, asking questions you don't want answers to."

Steel hardens even further, yet he tries to soften his tone, making it almost so he's pleading. "Maybe I do. Maybe I want to understand what's keeping you locked up in this prison of a house. What's keeping you locked away from yourself."

Reverie stands abruptly, her chair scraping against the floor. "You think this is a prison? You think you can waltz in here with your petty and naive curiosity and fix something that's been broken for lifetimes? You're a fool."

Steel stands as well, his tone firm but not unkind. "Maybe I am. But I'm here. You can't scare me."

Reverie's blue eyes blaze, her voice trembles with anger and something else—fear? Pain?

"Then you're an even bigger idiot than I thought."

She storms out of the dining hall, her footsteps echoing in the vast space. Steele stands there momentarily, running a hand through his hair, his heart pounding.

He picks up his half-finished glass of ale from the table and downs it in one gulp.

Edmund sidles up to him.

"You've known her for a while, haven't you?"

Edmund glances up at him, his gray eyes slicing as he clears some of the dishes. "I've served her for as long as she has needed me."

Steele frowns. "She doesn't seem the type to need anyone. Not that I'd say that to her face."

Edmund releases a faint smile that quirks up the side of his face, deepening his crow's feet. "Wise. She's endured much, more than you could imagine. Trust does not come easily to her—nor should it."

Steele crosses his arms. "So, how do I get her to trust me? I feel like every time I say something, I make it worse. If I'm to live here for eternity with you two and the ghosts, I'd like to be on good terms with the estate's monsters and the maiden who governs it."

Edmund pauses, meeting Steele's gaze with a measured look. "Trust is not something you gain with words alone, Mr. Steele. Actions speak louder, as they say. But it's not only what you do; it's why you do it."

Steele's bushy brows furrow. "What's that supposed to mean?"

Edmund resumes clearing the table and returns to the serving station. "She's not one to be swayed by grand gestures or hollow promises. She values consistency. Integrity. She watches for cracks in facades because she knows how easily they shatter."

Steel rubs the back of his neck, thinking. "So, what do I do? Just...exist near her until she decides I'm worth her time?"

Edmund smirks slightly. "It's a start. But more importantly, she needs to see that you're not afraid of her—not just the beast, but the woman beneath. And, Mr. Steele..." he leans forward slightly, his tone dropping to a conspiratorial whisper. "Be careful with her past. There are wounds there that are still bleeding. Show her you respect the scars without demanding to see them."

Steele nods slowly. "So, be patient. Be honest. And don't push too hard. Got it."

Edmund straightens, lifting the serving tray with the next course for Reverie with an effortless grace. "Precisely. But I'd also add a little humor occasionally, which wouldn't hurt. She hasn't laughed in years."

As Edmund turns to quit the dining room, Steele clears his throat. "Do you have anywhere in here that I can paint?"

Edmund turns, his white brows quirking up in curiosity. "Any one of the sitting rooms on your wing. Simply ask the house for supplies, and it will oblige."

Steele salutes him in thanks and downs the rest of his ale.

The need to release the storm of emotions swirling inside him becomes too great to ignore. Steele makes his way to a large sitting room he had discovered earlier, grateful for the lack of murderous encounters with the manor's more hostile spirits this time.

As he steps into the space, he looks around, hesitating momentarily before speaking.

"Um..." His voice feels awkward, almost absurd, directed at the empty room. "Can I have... a set of brushes, high-quality paints, a sketchbook, canvas, charcoal and pencils, palette knives, and an easel?"

A sudden whirl of bright, spinning light engulfs the room. Steele shields his eyes as the brilliance intensifies, accompanied by a gust of wind that sends loose papers and drapes fluttering. When the light finally dims, and the air settles, he opens his eyes to find everything he asked for neatly laid out before him, as if conjured from his thoughts.

He steps toward the stack of canvases propped against the stone wall, the light from the nearby window catching the pristine surface of the top one. Carefully, he lifts it onto the easel and settles onto the stool before it. He picks up a brush, dips it into the richly pigmented paint, and places the first stroke against the canvas.

At first, his movements are wild and chaotic, his emotions pouring out in raw, unrestrained strokes. But slowly, the frenzy gives way to form and purpose. Her eyes emerge from the chaos—those glowing embers pierce into his soul. Her fractured existence, beastly and human, takes shape in vivid, haunting detail.

Each line, each shadow, each color becomes an outlet for his turmoil, echoing the conflict he senses within her. The room soon transforms, the walls lined with paintings of her: fierce, vulnerable, radiant, broken.

Days bleed into nights as Steele immerses himself in his art, barely pausing to rest on the cot the manor conjured at his request. With a thought, food appears to sustain him, and even a bathroom materializes as if the manor itself anticipates his needs. Its magick becomes his refuge, allowing him to stay in his art room, crafting image after image of the mysterious being who both haunts and mesmerizes him.

On the eleventh day, as he works on yet another painting, a presence enters the room.

He doesn't notice at first, so consumed by his work. But when he hears the soft intake of breath, he glances up to see her standing in the doorway.

Reverie's eyes scan the room, taking in the countless depictions of herself. For a moment, her expression is unreadable. Then, slowly, a smile spreads across her face—a genuine, untarnished smile, as if for the first time in years.

Chapter Seven

REVERIE

Steele freezes, brush poised mid-air.

I don't know what I'd expected of him, yet he surprises me even more profoundly.

"I, uh—" he starts, but I hold a clawed hand at him, looking at the piece on his easel.

At first, I'm pissed.

A week and a half has passed since the dinner, and I've been so angry at him for trying to pry into my life—again.

Every curtain in my room was shredded to bits, only to be replaced and shredded again.

Staying to my wing and milling about my chambers, I only ventured into the main part of the house a few times. As soon as I heard the house stirring up things to frighten him, I returned to my quarters so I would not have to face him.

But this.

I hadn't expected this.

My eyes flit across the vast room Steele's been covering with pictures—pictures of scenery and landscapes, Hecate Manor, the village, the castle—but mostly, they're of me.

He stands as I move away from the easel, drawn to one across the room.

It's a charcoal depiction of me on the moors of the manor, hair blowing wildly in the wind, wearing the blue dress from the portrait hanging in the foyer. What's unique about this painting is the combination of color and charcoal. The features of my face and hair are elegant shading and penciling, but the dress is a brilliant, vibrant swirl of color with splashes of paint, and I'm looking into the sky, smiling.

I scrape a talon gently down the painting without leaving a mark—luckily the paints dry—and I can feel him hovering behind me.

Like patrons at an art show, I move quietly to each picture, looking at the detail.

It's like he's memorized every inch of me, the real me and he's only ever seen the one portrait in the hall.

He follows me quietly, almost timid, as though he's scared of my reaction to his artwork of me.

Another one depicts me mid-roar, fangs bared and claws out, but instead of terror or anger in my expression, there's...sheer indignation.

My brow furrows as I step closer to examine it, noticing the exaggerated details—the extra-fluffy mane of hair, the almost comedic way my claws are splayed. And then I spot it. He's added a tiny squirrel perched on my shoulder, looking as equally outraged, as though it's joining in on my tirade.

A laugh bursts out of me, sharp and unexpected, before I can stop it. "You gave me a backup vocalist?" I ask, turning to Steele, standing nearby with a sheepish grin.

"I figured you'd need some moral support during one of your epic rants," he says, his voice tinged with humor.

I shake my head, a slight chuckle still escaping me. "You're ridiculous."

But for the first time in what feels like an eternity, my anger starts to thaw, the absurdity of the drawing chipping away at my defenses.

"It was after four or five days of painting straight. I wanted to do something more light-hearted. I never intended for you to see them."

"Steele, these are great," I respond, moving from one to the next. Some are on canvases, and some are on paper, taped at odd angles on the walls. Not a space is clear of simple stone, but every inch is a colorful or intricate drawing of something. Even the pictures of the scenery are immaculate.

"Thanks," he replies, his voice curt, carrying the weight of unsaid words too vast to escape. His gaze locks onto mine, unyielding, his piercing eyes a molten shade of firewood, rich and consuming. Standing so close, I catch the faint scent of ale lingering on his breath.

"Painting calms me," he admits, his voice rough, like the tumble of stones down a mountainside. "It's a release. Everything inside me—every thought, every feeling—pours out onto the canvas, leaving me empty and... steady."

"I only have writing," I respond, my words smooth and low, drifting to him like the verses of a whispered song.

His gaze sharpens, probing as if searching for pieces of my essence buried deep within.

"What do you write?" he asks, his voice a quiet, weighty question that feels more intimate than it should.

Instead of recoiling away, I sink over to the table and sit, picking up an empty cup as it fills with ale. "I write poetry mainly. I've had ideas for stories over the years, but when I sit down to write them, they don't come out the way the novels in my library are written."

Steele goes back to the painting he was working on, and I watch him work. His wild tangle of curls is such a brilliant shade of mushroom brown in the dying afternoon light.

"Why don't you read books in the genre of the story you're trying to tell and take note of how the authors use their words?"

"I've tried," I admit, swirling the amber liquid around the pewter mug. "I still struggle with the in-between. I'm good with the important stuff, the intimate and meaningful scenes. It's the drivel between the important stuff I struggle with."

He nods imperceptibly, lost in his own creation. My eyes find an intimate portrait across the room, almost hidden behind another canvas. It's of a mother and baby, and it's definitely not me who's depicted in the image.

It's so intricate, a woman lying in bed, done solely in charcoal. She has long, dark hair and looks down lovingly at the babe wrapped in a blanket. As I reach the drawing, I'm swept away into that room as though witnessing the intimate moment between mother and newborn baby. It's so detailed that I am sure it's a memory and not his imagination gone wild—like most of the images of me.

Steele glances up from his work, catching sight of me studying the portrait. For a moment, his hand freezes, the brush hovering just above the canvas.

"That one..." he begins, his voice softer than I've heard before, almost reverent. He sets down his brush and wipes his hands on a rag as he walks over to me, his movements slow, deliberate.

"That's my wife," he says finally, his gaze fixed on the image as though seeing it anew. "And our son. She... they both died."

The words hang in the air, heavy and raw. I glance up at him, his face unreadable but his eyes betraying the depth of the wound he still carries.

"I'm sorry," I whisper, feeling the moment's weight pressing down on us.

He shrugs, a small, pained smile tugging at the corner of his lips. "It's been years. Painting them helps. Keeps them with me in some way, you know?"

I nod, unsure of what to say. The vulnerability in his voice and the love captured in that image tell me more about him than he likely realizes.

"What happened? If you don't mind my asking."

He glances up at me, impaling me with his cool, blazoned

stare. "I could say that I do mind you asking since you share so little of yourself with me. But I'll make you a deal."

I cringe, knowing what he is going to ask of me. I move away from the drawing, but he grasps my arm, and suddenly, I'm caught off guard by him.

My self-guarded armor dissolves. His eyes harden on me like molten ore dropped in a bed of snow. "What is your deal, sir?"

He pulls me over to the couches situated next to the fire. "I tell you a bit of my story; you tell me a bit of yours."

Chapter Eight

STEELE

STEELE FEELS HER SIMMERING FRUSTRATION, heavy and electric, like a storm cloud swelling and thickening the air with static tension.

Her bushy, furry brows hike up to her forehead, like the thoughts threading through her mind are too big—a swirling maelstrom of emotions spelled to be tethered to her bones.

"Alright," she concedes, scrunching herself up on the couch.

It's easy to see the woman inside the beast.

In fact, if Steele looks hard enough, he sees just that.

He inwardly asks the house to project her as she is inside, and the beast transforms before his eyes.

The maiden within is sitting next to him on the couch, her skin the soft color of caramel and her eyes a dark blue of a midnight sky.

She doesn't know that he is seeing the true her at this very moment.

Steele's breath catches, and he wonders if the manor's magick is somehow amplifying the gravity of her presence—or if it's just her.

The woman beside him leans back, her nails flexing absent-mindedly against the cushion, unaware that he's no longer seeing the beast but her true form. It's like something from a fairy tale, yet it's real.

She's real.

Her lips move, and he blinks, realizing he hasn't heard a word she's said.

"What?" he asks, voice hoarse. She flits back and forth in his vision, between the beast and the maiden—like she's glitching. He can see the maiden inside the beast, like the beast is a see-through armor.

"I said," she repeats, her frustration edging toward something softer, "are you going to keep staring at me like that, or do you have something to say?"

A faint smirk tugs at her mouth—a mouth that is both hers and not, as if the beast and maiden share the same sly humor. He feels the pull of her as if tethered by an invisible thread.

"You're beautiful," he murmurs, the words slipping free before he can stop them.

Her eyes widen, her claws retracting as if startled by the sudden intimacy of his tone.

"Beautiful?" she scoffs, but there's no anger behind it, only disbelief.

Steele leans closer, unable to help himself. "Yes. You are." His fingers brush against hers, and her breath hitches.

The tension between them thickens, a live wire sparking with possibility. His hand slides to her wrist, and he feels her pulse beneath his fingertips—rapid, strong, alive.

"You're not afraid of me," she whispers, her voice a mix of wonder and something deeper, darker.

"No," he replies, his lips so close to hers now that he can feel the warmth of her breath. "You make me feel more alive than I've felt in years."

Her claws rest against his chest, and for a moment, he thinks she'll push him away. But then, slowly, hesitantly, her fingers relax, sliding up to his shoulder.

When their lips meet, it's tentative at first—a question asked and answered. But as the moment deepens, so does the kiss, transforming from a gentle brush into something hungry and desperate, a collision of two souls both aching and afraid.

Her magick hums in the air, mingling with the crackling energy of the manor, and Steele feels it wrapping around them, binding them together in a way that feels fated and unbreakable.

Steele pulls back just enough to catch his breath, his forehead resting against hers. Her claws tremble against his shoulder, and for a moment, the silence between them feels sacred, a fragile thing neither wants to shatter.

But then, her gaze flickers, and she looks away, her expression haunted.

"I don't remember who I used to be," she says quietly, her voice raw, as if the words are being torn from some hidden part of her. "Not really. Bits and pieces, sure—a laugh, a feeling, the way sunlight felt on my skin. But the details?" She shakes her head, her claws curling into the fabric of his shirt. "They're gone."

Steele studies her, his heart clenching. He wants to ask, but the weight in her voice tells him to let her speak on her terms.

"Edmund... the manor... they remind me of my life before. A life I've spent years trying to forget." She exhales sharply, the sound almost a growl. "I've fought so hard to let go of who I was because it doesn't matter anymore. Not in this place. Not in this form."

"But why let go?" he asks gently, his fingers brushing against her cheek. "Wouldn't it be better to hold on to those pieces of yourself?"

Her laugh is bitter, almost mocking. "You don't understand. Those pieces—they're broken. Jagged. Every time I reach for them, they cut me to shreds. It's easier to just... exist. To be this." She gestures to herself, the beastly form that still shadows her true visage in his mind's eye. "This is all I have left now. The beast. The anger. The solitude."

Steele's thumb traces her jawline, his touch steady despite the storm of emotions raging between them. "I don't think that's all you have left," he says softly. "Not from what I've seen. Not from what I've felt."

Her eyes meet his, and for a moment, he thinks she might push him away again. But instead, she whispers, "You don't know the things I've done, Steele. The mistakes. The choices that led me here."

"Then tell me," he says, his voice firm but not unkind. "I'm not afraid of who you were. And I'm not afraid of who you are now."

Her lips part, but no words come out. Instead, a single tear escapes, glinting like starlight against her caramel skin before slipping down into the fur of her beastly form. Steele catches it with his thumb, his touch gentle, reverent.

"You don't have to be alone anymore," he whispers, leaning in to press a kiss to her temple. "Not with me. For the raindrop to join the rivers and oceans and become one with the earth again, it must first yield to the fall."

And with that, she falls.

She shatters.

She breaks.

He can feel her coming undone in his arms, unraveling before him with such ferocity that embers dance in the electric air around them.

Chapter Nine

REVERIE

I HAVE no idea what's come over me—or him, for that matter—because the way he's kissing me is more like he's making out with the most beautiful woman in the world.

The way he grabs the side of my face, like it's not laced with fur, and strokes my tongue with his like it's not being threatened to be sliced down the middle by my fangs.

When his hands trace stars around my scars, I gasp, and his rough, calloused hands find my breasts, rolling my pebbled nipple between his thumb and finger, creating a shudder that just won't stop.

He tucks a fall of inky locks behind my ear and mouths my neck, biting into my skin like it's not covered in fur, sending electric waves of glowing ghosts down my entire body.

He rips my tattered dress and throws it to the floor, peppering kisses down my body until he reaches my naval.

Even in my regular form, I wasn't a skinny girl—from what I can recall—but he sees no obstacles in my curves, treating my body as a treasure map he's destined to explore like it's his destiny to lay claim to my scars and map the constellations of my pain with his mouth.

As he dips lower to my clit, he looks up at me, the extended sharp features of his severe against my naked body. He looks like someone about to devour a four-course meal after being starved for days.

I taste smoke at the back of my throat as he tongue kisses my pussy, making me clench the cushions of the couch enough to rip into them, sending feathers flying into the air.

The gravelly moan crawling up his throat withers my mind to compost, the sort where bad decisions go to sprout. He adds fingers to his lustful meal, and I arch my back as I climb to the sun.

When he pulls me to the brink of release, he pulls his fingers free, dissolving my climax before it has the chance to curl over.

As he stands before me, the outline of his hard-on in his pants paints my arousal even brighter shades of want. I pull him toward me and rip his pants off, his giant cock springing to life before me. He removes his shirt, exposing his exquisitely defined abs and notches, pointing treasure hunters like myself toward the most delectable treasure.

Like coming upon the most delightful snack, my mouth salivates as I encircle the tip of his dick with my tongue, gazing up at him before sinking down the length.

Coaxing the most delicious sounds from his throat, I grasp him by his firm little ass and pull him into me as deep as I can. He grabs the back of my head and guides me fast, fast, slow, fast, fast, slow.

Every muscle in his body tenses up, and his dick hardens further when he pulls me from it to stop himself from cumming and kisses me, looking at me like I'm the one who shaped the sky.

He yanks me up from the floor and kisses me, then grabs me by the throat and throws me onto the couch.

Pulling my legs wide open, I feel on display until he says, "You're fucking perfect," as he swirls my clit with his thumb while the other hand guides himself into me.

"Oh fuck," I utter as he swirls his hips in one long roll, seating himself to the hilt within my depths.

I moan loudly, and he swallows the sound in a crumbling kiss, tasting my ruin at his hands like he has a sword notched at my neck.

In and out, he pierces me, peeling back my skin and exposing my ribs and inner workings—the maiden within the beast. The inner woman fights her way to the surface, peeling back the beastly layers and laying herself bare before this sexy man.

My claws rake over his pecs, the swirl of chest hair soft and rugged beneath my fingers. I'm careful not to claw him, but when I do scrape his skin more roughly than I intend, the guttural growl he emits lets me know it's a welcomed pain.

The air is thickening as we trade pieces of each other, and he pulls me with him when he reaches the edge of the universe.

The crescendo of ecstasy implodes me from the inside out, and as he explodes within, he kisses me like I am the last bit of air in a sinking ship.

As he slows his kisses and is about to pull out of me, the room grows unnaturally cold. The air crackles with energy, and the hearth flickers blue before dying out. The manor, alive with its own magick, responds to my anxiety. A heavy, gilded mirror on the far wall appears in the room before us and begins to glow, tapping into something within my memory.

"What the hell?" Steele mutters, removing himself from me and gathering his pants.

I freeze, my claws retracting as fear overtakes me. "No," I whisper. "Not this."

"What is it?" Steel asks me as he steps into his pants.

"My curse."

Chapter Ten

STEELE

THE MIRROR RIPPLES LIKE WATER, and suddenly, it shows a vivid, living memory:

It's dark in the halls of a grand castle. Steele watches as young Reverie runs in a white nightgown toward a young girl screaming. Moonlight dances through the rectangular windows, dappling the stone Reverie runs on. As she comes to a heavy wooden door with iron hinges, she bursts into the room to the dismay of the man assaulting the young girl.

Reverie screams, the man's wild gaze slicing through her, though he doesn't stop the assault on the girl. Reverie grabs a sword from the wall and runs up to the man, the crooked crown on his head introducing him as the king. The girl, face down in the four-poster bed, her nightgown hiked up, rendering her indecent, looks up at Reverie, her dark hair and features revealing that she's Reverie's younger sister. Reverie notches the sword at his neck.

"Let her go, or so help me god, I will tear you down the middle, then flip your insides to your outsides," she rasps, her words raw and stony.

The king's wild eyes go unfocused, and he mutters something

incoherently. He backs away from the girl as Reverie covers her and pulls her up.

The king, his crown sitting atop his head askew, is making himself decent again when a woman who looks like an older Reverie storm in—the queen.

Steele recognizes her from history books, though she looks young and beautiful.

The rumors of the kingdom's history are that the queen was cursed long ago, and while the kingdom further deteriorates, she's been cursed to rule the kingdom for eternity in her loneliness, forgetting about him and her daughters.

Steele is watching the curse as it happened so so very long ago.

The young Reverie stands before her sister, sword pointed at the king, while the queen assesses the situation. "What on earth is going on in here?"

"I told you, mother. I've tried telling you millions of times, yet you didn't listen," Reverie's face is red with anger, hot tingly tears streaming down her face. "The last time he did it to me, I nearly cut off his infernal, disgusting cock. He then turned to Seraphine. When I found out he was molesting my little sister and came to you, you did nothing to stop it then, either! So I swore the next time he did it, I'd kill him where he stands."

"He knows not what he does! He's sick with madness!" the queen defends him.

"Ah!" Reverie screams, her voice firm, defiant, as she runs towards her mother with the sword.

The king raises his hands, muttering an incantation, and in an instant, all three women are enveloped in swirling magick.

"You vile creature," he spits at Reverie, holding his bony hands up, magick sizzling between his fingertips like a neon web. "You will live as a beast!" the king roars. "A monster, unlovable and forgotten by all!"

Seraphine screams, running for her sister, but as she stumbles into the vortex of magick, her face goes blank, as does the face of the queen.

Reverie's body morphs into the being she is today, her skin coalescing into fur, her teeth into fangs, and the long black talons growing out from her fingers and toes.

Seraphine's body shrinks and morphs into a black raven with silver-tipped wings. The raven caws loudly before fleeing the room.

The queen's face falls as she forgets everyone in the room before her.

A puff of smoke blots out the light, and with it, the king evaporates.

Hecate Manor, at the edge of the village, erects itself out of the anger and rage wrung from the royals' wrongs, Reverie's emotions and despair painting everything in black and decay.

The vision shifts to the queen in her chambers, staring at a locket containing a miniature portrait of two young girls—Reverie and Seraphine. Tears stream down her face as she clutches the locket, muttering, "I had daughters, didn't I?" She falls deeper into despair with each passing day, unable to reconcile her fleeting memories. Her sadness weeps out into the village and forest, siphoning all the good, happiness, and health and plunging it into starvation and sadness.

The mirror fades, leaving Steele and Reverie in silence. Her beastly shoulders slump as though the weight of the memory is shattering her.

Silence reigns long enough to become uncomfortable, yet the weight of the realization crushes the awkward silence.

"That's why," Reverie says hoarsely, finally meeting his eyes. "That's why I wanted to forget. That's why I forgot."

The look on her face is a mixture of raw pain and echoing rage, fresh new agony seeping into her features.

Steele steps closer, his instinct to comfort warring with his disbelief. "But you remember. You're still here."

"I don't know if I'd call this living," she snaps bitterly, gesturing to herself. "I've been trapped in this form, this forest, for years. No one can save me. Not even you, Steele."

"Maybe," Steele says quietly, his jaw tight. "But maybe I can remind you what it means to fight for your own story again."

Chapter Eleven

REVERIE

I LET the power of his words seep into me, soothing the anger in my bones and accepting that I am and always have been part beast.

Maybe it's because of the trauma from my past, but it doesn't define me. It will forever be a part of me, but it's how I choose to wear the scars that matters. Yes, I am broken and shattered, but who's to say that trauma should map out the rest of my life?

I can live in harmony with the beast within me, for within the beast, there is beauty.

There's a resplendence within the broken.

An exquisite gold molding within the cracks of my past.

The manor shudders violently as the truth of my existence settles within my bones.

A low growl escapes my throat, sensing something ancient and familiar.

"He's here," I mutter, my claws extending. I pick my dress up from the floor and swoop it on, the seams magickally mending.

Steele retrieves his shirt and slips it on, buttoning it swiftly. "Who?" he asks worriedly.

Before I can answer, a cold wind tears through the room, setting all the papered artwork to the wind as it extinguishes every candle and the hearth's flame. The air is wicked from my lungs as the gilded mirror cracks, the fractured surface emitting the shadowy figure of my father, the king. His twisted, half-mad face emerges from the frame, stepping down from whatever nefarious plane he whisked himself to. The wicked smile splits his face, and his eyes glow unnaturally.

"My little beast," he sneers, his voice dripping with venom. "I see you've found a new companion to toy with."

Again, the rage returns with a vengeance, and I spring to my feet, positioning myself between my father and Steele. "You should've stayed in whatever pit you crawled into."

A laugh ricochets outward from the king's twisted mouth, reverberating like swords clashing. "And miss seeing how far you've fallen? No daughter. I've come to finish what I started."

The air grows oppressive, and Steele struggles to stand as my father begins an incantation.

A snarl bubbling up from the deepest depths shakes me to my marrow as I rush at him, colliding with air that sends me sprawling into the wall, the breath shoved out of me as I land hard on my shoulder.

"You've wasted your time clinging to your humanity," the king taunts me as I struggle to stand. "You could have embraced your beastly nature and ruled this forest. Instead, you linger in shame, waiting for someone to love a monster."

"You want to talk about monsters?" Steele snipes, his voice surging with rage; the veins on his neck bulge out unnaturally as though he has a beast within himself. "She's more human than you'll ever be."

The king narrows his eyes at Steele. "And you. The fool who thinks he can save her."

My father raises his hands, dark magic swirling toward Steele.

I know that magick.

I've suffered its fate for centuries.

The roar I let loose could dislodge the mountains as I lunge forward, diving into the space between the king and Steele. The magick slams into me like a collision, and my monstrous form grows larger, more feral, as I absorb the full brunt of the curse.

"Reverie! What did you do?" Steele shouts from the floor, having fallen with the collision of magick.

"I won't let him hurt anyone else," I growl, my voice distorted, but desperation fuels my conviction.

I fully embrace my monstrous form and charge for my father again, my claws ripping through his skin like butter. Four slash marks tear through his clothes and flay his skin wide open, blood dripping onto the floor. The king falters but doesn't yield, his laughter echoing ominously.

"You can't fight what you are," he hisses, his mouth weeping more of the crimson color, blood painting his teeth red.

"I'm both the beast and the maiden," I spit venomously. "I'm strong and fierce and will murder those who hurt others. But I'm not what you made me. I made myself and chose to wear my trauma like war paint. The past does not define me. While it may weave painful stitches in the fabric of my being, it's only holding space for the rest of my patches that now make up the present future."

As I speak, the magick floating around us begins to swirl. My body sinks to my average height, the fur disperses into my skin, and my clothes morph back into the size that fits my body.

Orange, red, and yellow sparkles leave me and swirl into my father, freezing him where he stands. The king lets out a roar of frustration as his form begins to dissolve. Piece by piece, he joins the sparkling air like a sand statue in a wind storm.

"You think you can save yourself?" he sneers as his hands disappear. "You'll never escape what I made you."

A snow globe appears in my hands, empty at first, yet as the orange swirling air desiccates him, it shifts its stream into the globe and reassembles him within the glass dome. "You can never hurt me again, nor anyone else. For I curse you for eternity to be who you are. *You're* the monster. And you'll live forever in isolation with nothing to keep you company but your selfish, sadistic thoughts. And then, you'll devour your own soul into nothingness, and nobody nowhere will remember you even existed."

The king moves to say something, but the dissolve has reached his face. He withers into the globe, where nothing and no one can ever hear him again.

I collapse from the sheer exhaustion of working with unfamiliar magick.

Steele rushes over to me, pulling me into his embrace.

"You did it," he coos, cupping my face. "You beat your curse."

"We did it," I tell him, looking up into his campfire eyes. "You saw the beauty within the beast. It was because of you that I was able to see the real me, who is both. Equal parts beast and beauty."

My breaths abandon me as he kisses me in his arms.

"I saw you from the very first meet in your garden. Your beast has always been becoming on you."

Chapter Twelve

REVERIE

The sight of my sister nearly buckles my knees.

She walks in from the hallway, her beautiful form normal and unscathed.

We embrace each other fiercely for a long while and cry together, Steele sitting back and giving us space.

The sound of soft, shuffling steps interrupts our embrace, and I turn to see a person exuding familiarity.

Edmund, who's not Edmund, walks in, a beautiful woman in a flowing gown moving over to me. I know it's him by the white hair and steel gray eyes.

"Edmund?" I ask, my brows notched together at the top of my nose. "Is that you?"

"Yes, m'lady," she says, her steel gray eyes piercing into mine with familiarity. "In your curse, you knew me as grief and rage and anger or any of the feelings you chose to discard. Now I'm love and life and happiness. I'll always exist within you; I'm the living embodiment of the emotion you choose to feed."

"So you're not grief and anger and rage?"

"I am, but I just changed clothes. I'm love now."

"And what was the answer to your riddle you told me the day Steele arrived, dear sister? It's been plaguing me for months now."

"It's a secret." She winks.

First I think she means the answer is a secret she's not willing to tell.

But then I realize the answer is *secret* and I smile.

"What happened to mother?" she asks Edmund.

"The queen has died with the curse," Edmund states, a tray of refreshments suddenly in his dainty hands. "She belonged to the curse, sadness, desperation, and despair. Because you broke that curse, m'lady, it means you're the new queen."

Another mirror appears in the center of the room, projecting the castle and surrounding villages. The deep, dark, dying forest blooms into green, lush, and revitalized trees. The clouds looming over the village dissipate to a crystal blue sky, and the fields and crops blossom before our eyes. Happiness and laughter return to the people, and the blight that was the Great Hunger is lifted.

"So, what does this mean?" Steele asks again, accepting the ale offered by Edmund.

"It means," Edmund replies, offering a mug to Seraphine next, "that Reverie and Seraphine are now the reigning queens of the kingdom. And they may choose to rule however they see fit."

I look to my sister, the strong, fierce, loyal, and loving girl.

She was always the best of us.

"You rule the kingdom, Sera," I say softly, grasping her hands in mine.

She looks at me with disbelief. "What? Why me?"

"Because you are better for the job," I tell her. "We both know that you will rule the kingdom with love and light and bring us into the new era of lovely things. You've always been meant for the throne. Not me."

"What will you do?" she asks, her eyes filling with tears.

I look at Steele, whose molten stare singes me to my bones. "I don't know, maybe write a book."

He smiles, and something dislodges within me. I don't know what kind of life lies ahead. But I do know that meeting this man has changed me somehow. And while I learn to dislodge the ghosts from my heart, I intend to try and make room for him.

I'm blazing ice, and he's fractured fire. Together, we create steam and chaos, fated to unravel each other's shadows. His molten stare warms my fractured soul, and I know I'll burn beneath him, dissolving our demons, until the world crumbles around us. I'll willingly melt beneath him, even as the world collapses around us. And when it does, I'll rise from the ashes as I always have. But this time, I won't rise alone.

Steele reaches for my hand, his touch grounding me in a way I've never known. My sister's tearful smile assures me I'm making the right choice.

The kingdom will flourish under her reign, and I'll find my own path, one not dictated by curses or despair.

"Hecate Manor is home," he says. "Our home."

He impales me with another stare that promises me everything I want.

And for the first time, I'm free.

THE END

About the Author

Inara Gage is an indie author based in Northern Colorado. She resides with her son Gauge, her mastador Khaleesi, kitty Nox, and bunny tWitch. After the first two failures of publishing her first book, A Witch's Aura, she went all the way through grad school to learn how to market herself in this crazy, incredibly hard, and immensely trying self publishing world. This is her third book baby and she learned so much from all the trials and tribulations with the first one, she has authored five more books since and hopes to continue putting stories out into the world that you all will love and enjoy.

Also by Inara Gage

A Bond with the Dark

A Bond with the Blood of Angels

A Bond with the Wrath of Demons

A Witch's Aura

Aura's Dilemma